# A day with the Animal Firefighters

Sharon Rentta

Moose is very excited.
He's going to be a firefighter.
He's got a lot to learn . . .

. . . and he won't be allowed to drive the fire engine till he's got Experience.

In Basic Training, firefighters learn how to use all sorts of Special Equipment. They learn that fire extinguishers must never be pointed at other people . . .

. . . and that the hose often has a Mind Of Its Own.

Firefighters also learn to use Common Sense.
Common Sense is useful when you're
rescuing people.

I'm upside
down, Moose!

Apparently the safety net
is for catching people,
not for bouncing on.

After training, each firefighter joins a team called a Company.
This is Blue Company. They're going to work the Night Shift.

You can't be a firefighter
if you're . . .

too slow,

too silly,

too prickly,

or too fiery.

Moose joins Red Company. They will work the Day Shift.

They are all obviously Very Brave
– and they are all Ready for Anything.

They have 24 boots between them.

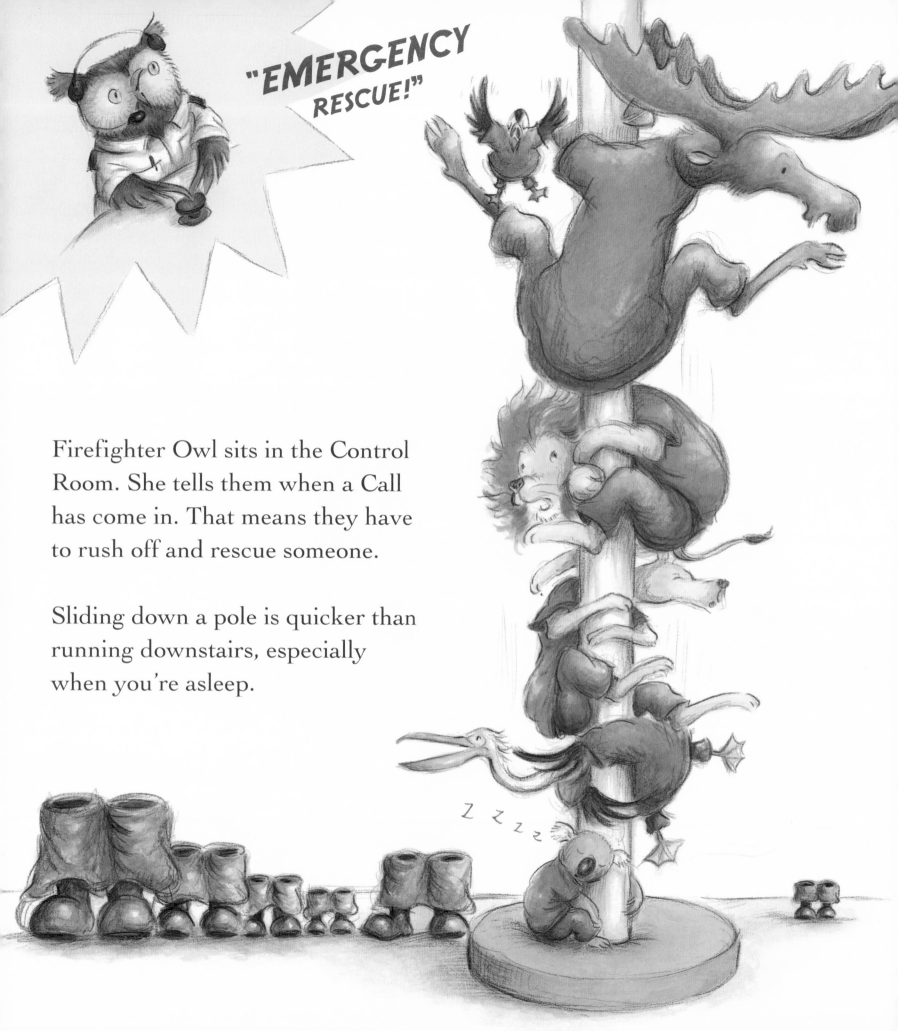

"EMERGENCY RESCUE!"

Firefighter Owl sits in the Control Room. She tells them when a Call has come in. That means they have to rush off and rescue someone.

Sliding down a pole is quicker than running downstairs, especially when you're asleep.

Z Z z z

Moose learns to get ready
in Double-Quick Time.

Personal Protective
Equipment is very heavy.

Firefighters have to wear a lot
of Personal Protective Equipment.

oxygen
tank

goggles

gloves

helmet

boots

oof!

In just two minutes, the firefighters are ready to go.
Moose still isn't allowed to drive the fire engine . . .

. . . so he just shouts "Nee-naw! Nee-naw! Nee-naw!" as they drive along. This isn't strictly necessary, but it's fun.

Firefighters don't just tackle fires.

Here, a baby critter has gotten stuck on a tall giraffe.

This ostrich is
trapped in a drain.

Dachshunds sometimes
get stuck up drainpipes.

And they often have to
pull a pig out of a pothole.

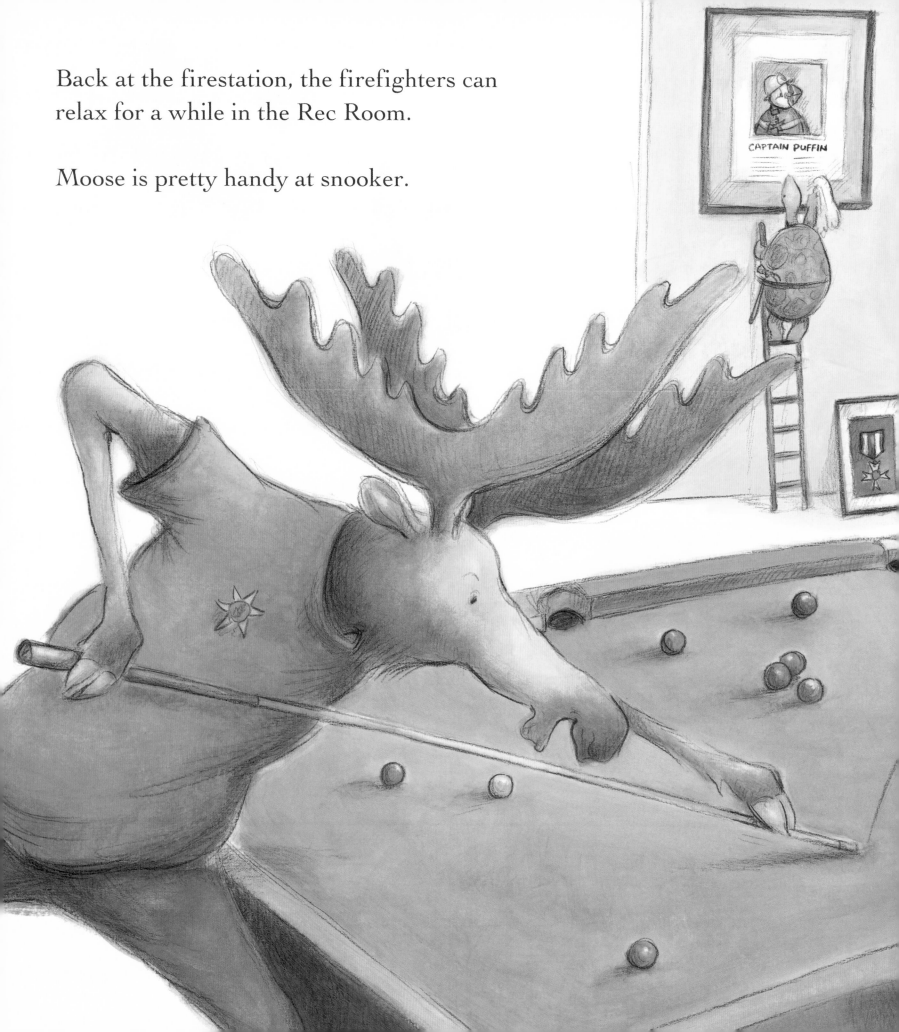

Back at the firestation, the firefighters can relax for a while in the Rec Room.

Moose is pretty handy at snooker.

CAPTAIN PUFFIN

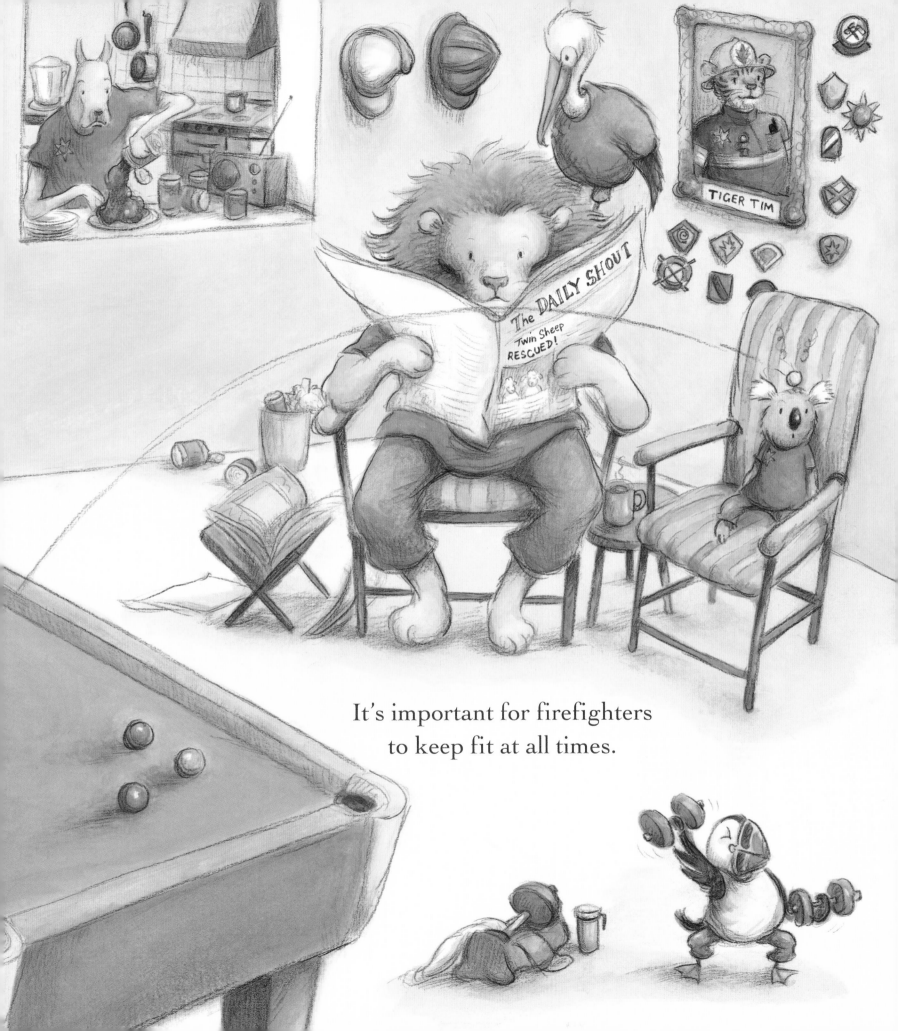

It's important for firefighters
to keep fit at all times.

Firefighters take turns doing the cooking. Today it's Firefighter Dog's turn.
He tends to just open a can of something.

No one's very keen on Dog's dinner.

"EMERGENCY!
32 WARREN LANE!"

Luckily there isn't time to eat it.
The alarm goes, and it's Action Stations.
They're off to the rescue again!

For this rescue, the firefighters need their Breathing Apparatus.

Some skunks have let off a really stinky smell next to some rabbits.

*Swoon!*

The rabbits have fainted – but they will
be fine after hospital treatment.

So will Firefighter Koala, who wasn't
quite quick enough with his gas mask.

Oops!

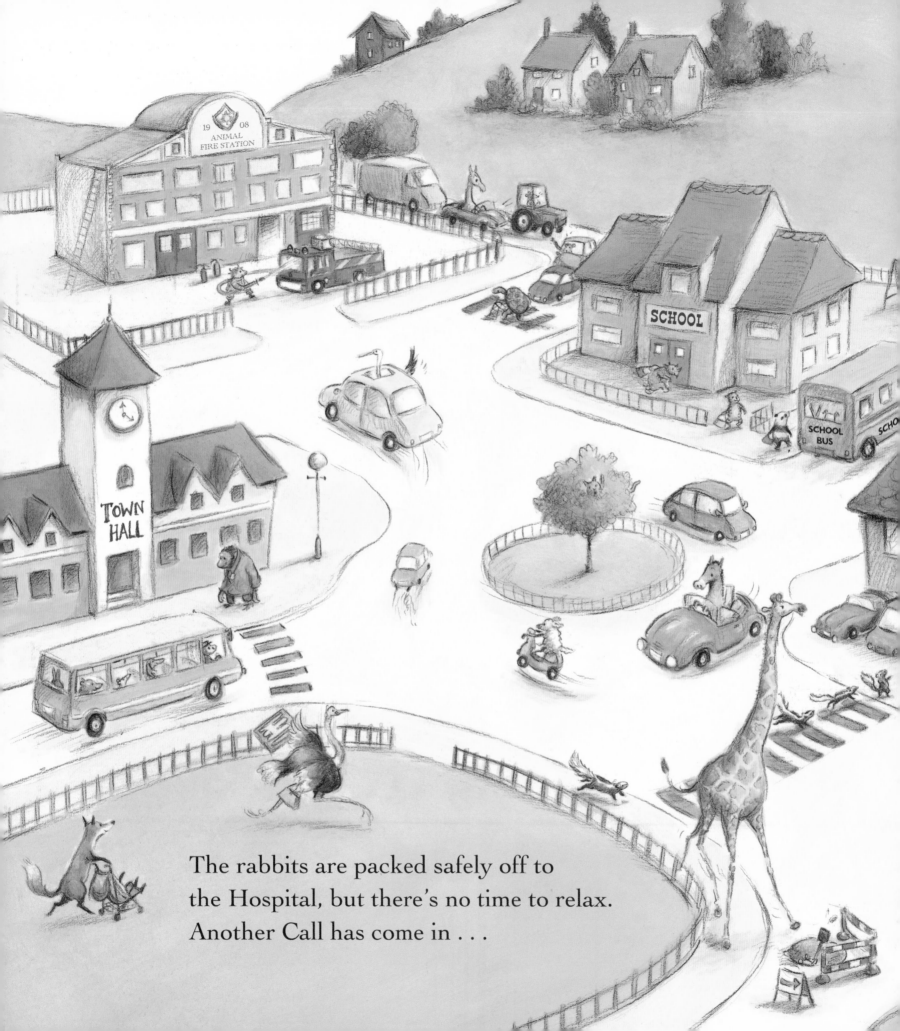

The rabbits are packed safely off to
the Hospital, but there's no time to relax.
Another Call has come in . . .

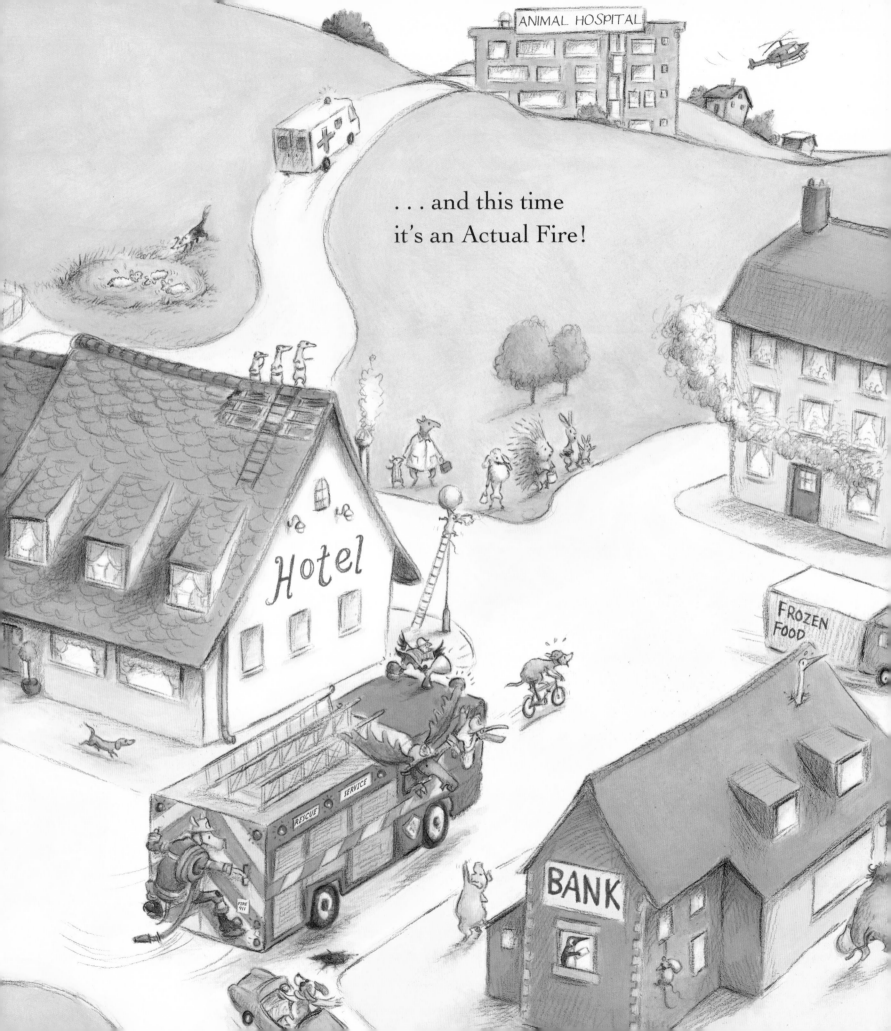

. . . and this time
it's an Actual Fire!

Station Officer Puffin quickly sizes up the situation.

It was Grandpa Tortoise's 249th birthday.

That's a lot of candles to have on a cake . . .

. . . and they set fire to the decorations!

The firefighters quickly rescue the tortoise family . . . but what about the twenty-one guinea-pigs on the top floor? They're too scared to jump, and it'll take too long to rescue them one by one!

Then Moose has a Bright Idea . . .

While the rest of the
Company tackle the fire,
Moose bravely climbs
the ladder . . .

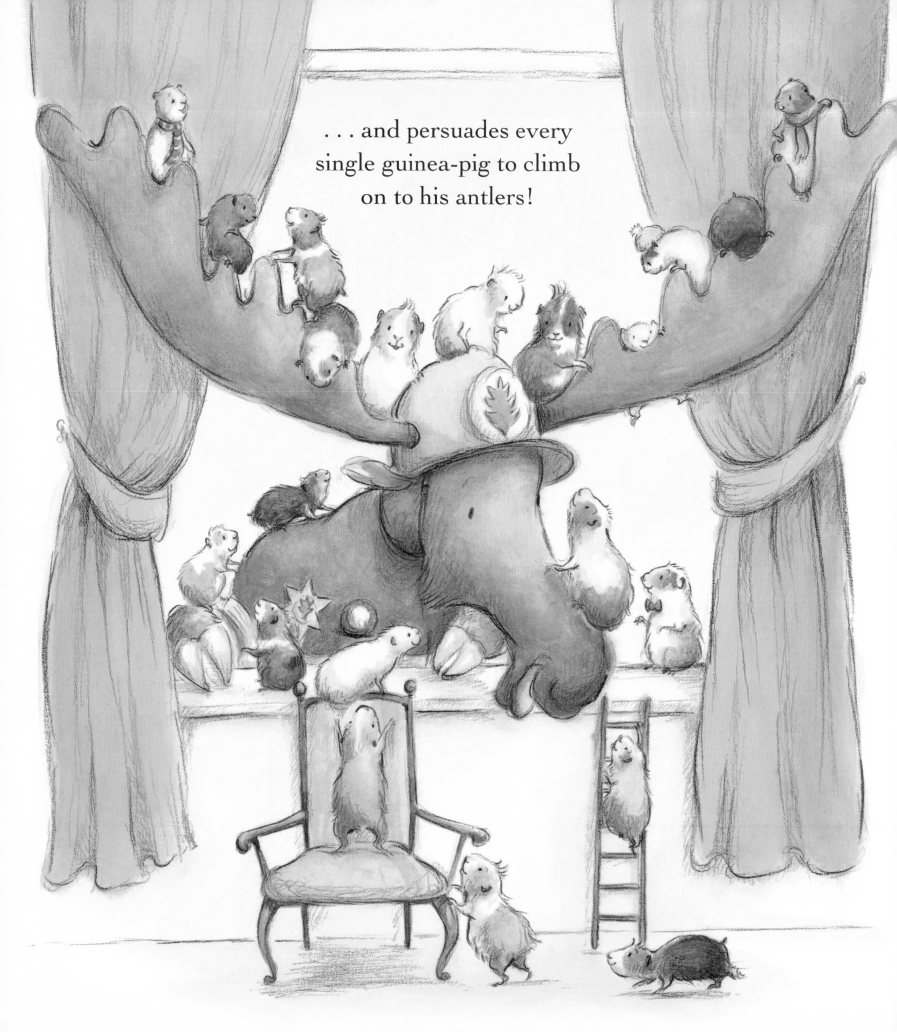

. . . and persuades every
single guinea-pig to climb
on to his antlers!

What a hero!

Everyone agrees that Moose has demonstrated Bravery and Quick Thinking.

Station Officer Puffin
awards him a medal.

And at long last . . .

Thank you,
MOOSE!

. . . he's allowed to drive the fire engine!
Congratulations, Firefighter Moose! Excellent work!

For Firefighter Peter and
also all the Firefighters at
Euston Fire Station.

First published in 2012 by Alison Green Books
An imprint of Scholastic Children's Books
Euston House, 24 Eversholt Street
London NW1 1DB
A division of Scholastic Ltd
London ~ New York ~ Toronto ~ Sydney
Auckland ~ Mexico City ~ New Delhi ~ Hong Kong

Copyright © 2012 Sharon Rentta

ISBN 978-1-4351-4869-7

Manufactured in Malaysia
Lot #:
9 8 7 6 5 4 3 2
April 2014